FINDING

YOGENDRA NIKALE

written by : yogendra nikale.

tittle : finding.

it was midnight.

there were 3 different ships. one from russia, one from china and one from uk .

in these ships there were young children, girls and men. their hands were tied from a rope. and they were in a metal cage.

jeni was in the prisoner in the ship of uk. there was a small child there with the comics.

jeni asks for the comic and tears the last page and starts carving.

in the docks of usa. this prisoners were removed from their cells and gathered.

the bad guys were sperating the men, children and girls from each other.

one girl makes a boy run and he runs and one of the bad guy shoots the boy and also the girl.

dang was the leader.

dang : anyone who makes a run for will die the same way. [dang had a russian accent]

the bad guys started putting masks on them. and their hands were also tied backwards.

one guy on walky : send in the trucks.

three trucks came.

now there were three different groups. men, girls and children. they all were loaded in three different trucks.

the girls truck driver is john.[wearing red cap]

john watches from his side mirror girls were getting loaded.

a masked guy with a machine gun watches him and john looks him and john notices a tatoo above his fingers of a lizard .

the tattoo guy : what are you looking at [russian accent]

then john looks in the front. as if he has seen nothing.

when the loading was done they got their destination.
one guy with gun and wearing a black mask sits in johns truck beside him and he told him to move
and the truck went 3 different ways.
jeni was a prisoner in the truck of john. her mask little torn off so she could see.
the truck stopped at a big mansion.
they started emptying the truck there.
jeni saw the sticker on the truck.
they were taken in the mansion. forcefully. they were still masked.
they were taken in the dungeons, jenny watches the way she came in.
she also watches a dead girl getting being taken away to the dump
what ever the bad guys do from dang is ordering them.
the bad guys stop them, they start giving them the drug with a needle.
dang :: keep it low they might die from a first dose. [to the guys giving drugs]
the bad guys uncover their mask, untie them. they all are in a drug trip even jenny.
there was also a hot stell sword to stamp them.
dang : you girls are our property now, you will eat when we decide, you will rest when menn are satisfied, if you want to live dont struggle, or you have seen the concequences.
jeni pisses in her pants right there standing.
dang : ohh gosh. put them inside. and prepare for stamping [watching the hot rod in the fire]
the bad guys put them in dungeons.
cut to
frank stops the truck on the street way back home. and shouts hruhhhhh and breaths heavily. looks at his fathers picture and calms down. and starts drinking.

jeni is drugged her visions are blurry and finds a tooth brush in the dungeon she breaks

the watcher of the dungeons : ohh crap what a bad smell.

the watcher takes the mob and the bucket for cleaning. and was about to clean he watches jeni.

watcher : you crap you did mess you are gonna cllean it up. [while saying this he starts opening the door of the cage and pulls jeni from her hair and brings her out.

watcher : your piss, you clean it.

jeni gets up and turns.

watcher : didnyou hear what i said bitch.

jeni puts the broken tooth brush in his neck.

cut to

jeni comes out. she knows the way. her head is spinning. she is under the trip of drug but still she is running and getting out.

cut to

one chines girl from the cage watches the door cage door open. she comes out. she watches the watcher is struggling to breeath and blood from his neck.

she starts walking but she goes in a different direction where dang is.

jeni comes out of the dungeon and clims the fence. the fence had glass spikes, she gets stabbed on her hand and legs comes down on the other side and starts running on the street. she is getting her concious back.

cut to the chinese girl goes near dang.

dang was talkingg to his boss.

dang : yes boss, in 5 min will leave for the children section.

the girl watching dang turns back.

dang shouts hey hey ! annd run towards her. he catches her and grabs her arms.

dang : how did you get, how did you get out?

the girl answers nothing, dang runs towards the dungeon. he watches the watcher on the floor and struggling to breath.

the watcher raises his hands help me help me.

dang watches the prisoners and stamps on the head of watcher. and runs out with his badguys.

jeni is running on the street and falling here and there. she watches a truck on the street. jeni shouts help. help

john watches her from the mirror. she comes closer to the truck she recognizes the sticker from of the truck.

john comes out of his truck and watches her.

she leaves the street sayinng no no. and runs in the bushes.

dang takes a torch wacthes the fence there was blood on it and runs towards the street.

jeny is now reached in the jungle .

dang is following the blood on the street. and he follows till the jungle.

john suddenly hold her from back.

jeni says no, no,

john : dont shout. [points at dang with his guy] dont shout.

dang shouts : any sign of the bitch.

one bad guy screams : no nothing. [they run searching far from john and jeni]

after watching them go jeni starts speaking.

jeni : i did nothing, i seriously did nothing. i was in the school. i came home back in the afternoon. people grabbed me in my own house. i did nothing, i swear to god i did nothiing.

john : i know

jeni : then help me please help me. here this is where i live take it [she removes the comic last page and gives him] please imform my dad. he stays here he will tell you. who i am.

john : what your name.

she tells her name

john : jeni look, i am gonna go now.

jeni : no, no, no, dont leave me here, take me with you

john : i said listen to me. those guys are near my truck. if i take you they will kill me and catch you. you hide here, i will be back here in dawn.

jeni : no, no, no,

john : listen to me jeni its the only way. i will be back in the morning. and im gonna take you and help you go home. just hold tight.

john goes near the truck and davee stops him. jeni is watching them from the jungle.

dave : whats did you stop.

john : i stopped to piss.

dave : check his truck. [the guys check his truck and says he is clean]

john : im the guy dropped your package rememeber.

dave : just get the fuck out of here. [he continues watching from torch in the jungle]

john looks back at him and the girl and gets in the truck and leaves

john goes in a bar near the docks.

he drinks and he watches the time and the bar woman watches him.

in sun rise he goes at the spot. jeni is not there.

he see's finger marks on the mud. [he visualizes she is been dragged]

he looks here and there

and the tittle finding.

bad dream of william getting tortured.

willliam wakes up screaming in anger, looks here and there. watches the picture of his wife and daughter. he calms down. and watches a cat staring at him . gets up from the bed. looks in the mirror his scars on the body.

cut to

jogging on the street. long jog.

came home back, taking juice from the refrigerator.
wife calls: hi honey how's you.
william : fine lady, how's our girl.
wife : girl is fine, shee is sleeping now. she keeps on asking you. when you are gonna come home. what do i say her.
william : i dont know. eli. i just dont know
wife : its been 6 months you been living in that house alone, why are you punishing yourself. forget it. forgive yourself.
william : i dont want you guys to be victim of my anger.
wife : again the same thing, there are professional people who can help you, therapies are there and even anger mangement programs are there.
william : yeah i'll think about it,
wife : stop pushing us away will. if you want we can come there and live with you.
william : [yells] i said no. no [breaths and then calms down] listen i have to first be little social. go out work somewhere. get into habbit of being normal with everyone. im not enjoying this, but its for your own good.
wife : do what is best for you william dont think of us. [william cuts the phone and his wfe cries]
her girl wakes up : mommy, why are you crying. did you speak with daddy [elli wipes her tears and goes towards her]
wife : no, it was not daddy.
girl : then why are you crying.
wife : i was not crying, i was just exited for weekend because we are going to the circus again.
girl : yeah the clown, ape and the lion show. [and she hugs]
cut to
interview
william went to shop in mall.

he buy's stuff very normally.
he doesnt talk to anyone.
he watches a wall sticker. wanted painter.
he also works as painter but never talks witth anyone.
he sits on his chair drinks and pass outs.
his neighbour old lady watch him but he never speaks
one day
a small child fires crackers on the street. and will was sleeping.
the cracker blows and will wakes up.
the boy latter puts fire cracker in the williams mailbox
will comes out of his house to see what is the sound .
the boy runs after watching will.
and the fire cracker blows.
will watches the kid run. and he goes near the gate where the mailbox is fixed and looks there are letters.
he warches his neighbours are staring him. he stares back right and left and lso the car and get back home
he starts opening the letters
there were 7 letters every letter was the same.
the letter say's
hello dad , this is jenny please save me, i am in pensylvania , i am caged against my will, please set me free.
william reads this and keeps on the desk.
he starts searching the house.
his wife calls he picks up and says i will call you back.
and searches the entire house. he finds nothing. he checks the attic he finds a picture.
the picture has 2 children and parents.
he comes out with the picture. and breaths heavy.
his neighbours watches him. he goes near the old lady neighbour
will : can i speak with you for minute.

old lady : yes.
will : i found a picture. in my house. is the girls name jenny.
old lady wears her glass : no thats martha and robin. children of mr. and mrs smith. they used to live in your house few months back.
will : yes they sold the place. but do they used to call her jenny.
old lady : no they used to call her by her name martha. but why you are asking.
will : i saw letters in my mail box. they are from usa send to my address. i dont know what to make out of this.
old lady : this might be the children who play around here , they do lot of mischief. dont you worry the girl in photo her name is martha.
will stares at her and then to the letters.
cut to
william is taking stuff in the mall,
he putting his esentials in his tray.
he was passing by with his tray and in front of him teen age kids were taking pictures, he stops so he shouldnt come in between. as they took the picture he passes.
he watches a long queque at the cash counter, one is working hard . and another cash counter is closed the man is talking on the phone from behind and a man comes and his tray dashes him from behind.
the man says : im sorry
william turns back and says "why dont you just kill me with that tray.
thhe man : i said im sorry.
william turns his tray towards him and dashes his tray again and again and shouts sorry, sorry, sorry.
william had the entire mall's attention.
and starts breathing heavy.
there comes the manager : sir is there any problem.
william : this mall has a problem. there are kids around hopping and taking pictures.there is such a long queue and still the boy has closed

his cash counter because he is busy talking.
the man in front take my spot sir come.
william : no thank you [and calms down]
william starts breathing heavy.
the boy starts the cash counter and says, the counter is open sir, you can come here.
william looks behind and the man who dashed him, he watches him and says after you sir im sorry. the man says thank you very and im sorry once again.
cut to
phone with his wife.
wife : just remove it from your head. you neighbour told its nothing the girls name is martha. the kids are messing around.
will : yeah i figgured.
wife : just stop thinking about it ok, take care of your self.
william keeps the phone and drinks.
william sitting on the chair and drinking and he passes out, he starts getting visions of his past. then he watches his girl in the blood and sound dad help me dad iam caged. please help me . suddenly he gets up. and looks at his family picture and then he pics smith's family picture and drinks a sip
cut to
next day in the morning he goes to the neighbour's house with flowers. she was inside the house, the door was open and a transperant shutter was there.
old lady : who is it ?
will : mam its me your neighbour. i want to talk to you.
old lady goes near the door opens the shutter. come in come
will comes in and gives her the flowers
old lady : ohh thank you, come sits on the chairs
her grandchildren were playing video games. and making lot of noice

old lady : go upstairs for a while we need to talk

the children : what grandma you always do this.

old lady : my grand children, very loud they are.

child from upstairs: not loud than you grandma.

old lady : shut it, other wise no vedeo games for a week.[then she looks towards the will]

old lady : tell, what you want to talk about .

william : according to the letters. the first letter was sended to me was in november. and i moved in this house in february. when did the smith family left this house. beacuse i never met them because i bought from the agency.

old lady : they celebrated christmass over here, and they left in jan first week. i dont remember the date.

william : was their girl with them.

old lady : yes she was here, and was very happy too. oooh i get it now, you are too much worried for the child. i told you its nothing. it might be the kids.

william : madam, one more thing i want to return some stuff, they left some stuff in the house. i want to return them. can you tell me where they live.

old lady : they live right here in nothingham. i dont know the exact adress but mrs smith gave mme a note once.

she starts checking for the note.and she finds its.

lady : here it is, take it. one more advice. when i look at you , i feel there is something wrong with you, i dont know what it is, get back to your family before its too late, beacuse when lonliness gets your head, the light keeps on fadding and the darkness takes over.

cut to

william to way to notingham in a taxi, he starring outside.

taxi driver : this is the place mate.

william rings the door bell of mr. smith in nothingham.

mr. smith answers : yes.
william : i live in your house in cambridge. [mrs smith watching from behind]
mr. smith : its not my house anymore.
wiliam : i know i bought it.
mr. smith : what brings you here.
william : i found your picture in the house. i came to return it.[gives him the picture]
mr. smith : [takes the picture] how thoughtfull of you.
willliam : there is something else. do know anyone maned jenny. [his wife reacts shocking]
mr. smith : no, i dont know anyone named jenny [and looks back to his wife] why you ask.
william : because someone is been sending mails from november at my house from usa . does this mean anything to you
mr. smith : takes the letter reads it and and "says nothing, not a clue " [martha comes near mrs. smith and says please zip my dress from my back and mrs smith is zipping it and williiam watches it]
mr. smith : is there anything else[will watches his daughter martha and nods his head to mr smith] anyways thanks for the picture [and shuts the door]
cut to
william : calling to his wife in cab while reaching home. [night]
wife : i cant believe you went there. i thought you must have forgoten it
will : i dont know , i just wanted to do it, to make sure ....
wife : to make sure whaether the girl is fine. we have enough of our own problems will.
will reaches his house from his cab. he passes from his house and watches the old lady at her porch. he tells the driver to stop the car. and he cuts the phone.

wife : i hate him when he does that.
will throws the money to the cab driver and comes out in rush towards his house eneters his gate and watchhig him the old lady stands up.
old lady : there is something i want to tell you. i dig down into my old memories and there is one night which always made me wonder. what is it all about.
will : what happened ?
old lady : 3 years back, one lady older than smith came to his house crying. i was watching it from my porch. mr. smith was hidding something from his wife. he took her near the gate and was making her calm. they were too far i couldnt hear them. he was whispering and lady gave him some papers and he hugged her and took her to the car. and she left. i wonder what was on that papers.[visuals of the flashback]
old lady : [starts leaving from there] i thought there might be something behind this or may be nothing. ii thought you should know.
will : watches he go and looks towards his house and his gate.
cut to
will siiting in his chair in his house and drinking.
cut to
[its evening]will starts stalking on mr. smith. mr. smith goes out. he rings the bell. of the house. mrs smith opens the door and watches will.
mrs smith to will : mr. smith is not home.
will : i know, i saw him going. its you i want to meet. you know someone named jenny.
mrs smith shuts the door but will stop from his hand.
mrs smith : i dont know anyone.
will : then why do i get a feeling, you know something. if there is any jeny, she is caged . and she is begging her father to relase her.

mrs smith : starts crying.
will : please mrs. i need your help.
mrs smith : alright, come in.
will enters thhe house and they both sit.
mrs smith : howard my husband had a relationship with someone before our marriage. he didnt marry the girl but he was the father of her child. after meeting me he left her and vanished. but 3 years back she started finding him. and one night she reached at our house, i wash watching from the window.
flash back visuals
mother banging on the door of howards shoulting "howard, howard"
mr. smith opens the door and takes her near the gate.
and mrs. smith watching them from the balcony wiindow.
mother : you left me howard, you left me.
mr. smith : im so sorry, i had no other option.
mother : after all this years i came searching for you because im going to die. i have cancer. i need someone to take care of our child.
mr. smith : but how its possible, i got my own family.
mother : she is also your family. this are the house papers. the house is yours just take care our child.
mr. smith : takes the papers and hugs her and takes her towards the car and she leaves
mr. smith eneters his house.
mrs. smith : who was the lady howard
mr. smith : it was just someone in trouble. so bought their house. let me finih my dinner.
mrs. smith : he lied to me, i heard everything, i knew everything. but we never spoke of it. [visuals howard eating dinner]
the woman died last year, all she ever wanted someone trustworthy to take care of her child. who can it be than her father. so she gave this house and the child in the hands of howard. and that child's

name is jeny.
will starring at her.
mrs smith : and when the mother died we moved in here. but there is no sighn of the girl. i never even saw her. thats alll i know, i swear to god. thats it. [starts crying]
will : yes i trust you. do you have any picture of jeny. yes i do. the
mrs smith : yes i do, when we moved here. there were pictures in the attic. i figured it was jenny[she gives him the pictuere]
will takes it
mrs. smith : please free the poor child, where ever she is free her no matter what it takes.
will : stares at the lady.
cut to
[its night]will coming out of her house. and mr. smith watches him coming out.
cut to
william digging in front of his house.
the old lady : whats the grave for.
william : its not a grave i want to make a pool out here.
old lady : keep up the good work.
cut to
will is all mudy and in his house drinking on his chair . and his wife is on the call.
wife : ohh my god this is really unhuman, now get into any kind of trouble, go to the police and tell them what you know. [suddenly a sound comes]
wife : whats that sound.
will : it might be the cat, she keeps hopping around. i'll call you back.
will takes the gun from the drawer and tug it in his boots. and comes down stairs. he watches around, its dark and looks it his door, the door was open. then goes towards the light switch and turns, mr.

smith with a rod knocks him down
cut to
vision of the past
william wakes up and his hands are tied on a chair. and he has a bruise on his head.
he watches 2 guys are putting petrol in his house. and mr. smth watches him getting concious.
mr. smith to william : wakie wakie. tell me. what did you speak about to wife in my house.
william : i want to know about the girl.
mr smith : who are you anyways, to find her. you couldnt sleep well, you have anger issues, you fight with everyone. so you can clean your slate. by being a hero.
william stares.
mr. smith : what do you think i dont know about you. i have ears buddy. we all are monsters, tthe only thing is you are uncovered. how you like this story angry mad man burn down the house and dies in his own flame.
william : what did you do with the girl.
mr. smith : the girl , the jeny my beloved daughter. i couldnt kill her. and i couldnt bring her into my family either. so i sold her.
william : what kind of father you are.
mr. smith : im not her father. who told you that. jeny's mother was mentally unstable. jeny was born before i met her mother. i was homeless and weak. so i did my with her. but when the time came i left her. i did what i had to do for survival.
william : what the poor child did to you.
mr. smith : who would believe, she is not my child. come one you tell me yourself. do you believe me. throwing her out was the only option left.
william takes his left foot on his knees and tries to move his jeans

from the bottom to reach at the gun tugged in the boots.
william : when i was upstairs, i heard a noice down and i knew someone broke in and i knew it was you.
mr. smith : so what did you do about it.
william : you spoke about monsters, you havent seen the real monster yet.
removes his gun from the boot and shoots through his tied hands . the bullet hits his ear of mr. smith. and he shoots both of them in the chest.
mr. smith runs from there. william tries to untie him from his mouth. smith goes near the car he realizes he has no keys. and he starts running on the street holding his bloody ear.
william unties his one hand and gets up kicks the other handle of the chair and in 2 kick the handle brakes. he remove his hand and runs out for the smith.
he runs and yells hey you mother fucker. he fires 3 rounds and he drags mr. smith towards his house
cut to
he puts mr smith in the hole digged in front of his house.
he eneters the house watches one guy was struggling to get up. he shoots him twice [shooting shot is outdoor shot.]
cut to
william has burried 3 of them in the front of his house. and was leveling the ground with the square shovel. its morning.
the old lady comes out her house and from her porch she watches william levelling the ground.
the old lady : hey where's the pool.
will : change of plans, i have to go to america for a holiday. maybe i'll swim in the beach.
old lady : last night i heard, gunshots.
will : i heard too, as you told it might be the children. [and he smiles]

old lady : you look happy.
will : yeah kind of feeling after soo many years.
cut to
will traveling in plane. watching outside in window . [day time]
william on airpaot shots
william on escalator shots.
will comes out of airport and his wife calls.
at night lands in pensylvania. in the airpport his wife call "i been trying to get to you for hours where are you. "
will : i toook a flight to pensylvania. just landed.
wife : tell me this is not about the girl. i told you do a police complaint of that man.
will : he is dead.
wife : ohh my god, what have you done. you just go and killl people for their crimes. next you are gonna do what, find the girl kill anyone who comes in between.
will : yes.
wife : yes, then what about us, what about our girl. there might me a big mob involved, do you think me and our daughter can fight them. tell me.
will : dont worry, no one will come after you, even if i die here trust me on this. [[keeps the phone]
wife after keeping phone : what fuck this is man is gonna now.
will opens his cell phone breaks his sim, and throws, brakes his mobile and throws in the public dustbin
william walks further and stops where no one is around and he burns his passport. but a beggar watches him.
beggar to william ; i have seen people burning lot of things, but the man who burns his identity is gonna burn down the town.
take prints of the jenny's photograph and keeps it in his jacket. from a photostudio.

will catches a cab and says take me to the nearest brothel .
taxi driver : someone is really loaded.
will : just dont ask.
taxi driver drives.
taxi driver drives.
he watches the streets and its activities, he watches hookers on the street. people robbing people. poliice catching people. dark places.
the taxi driver stops near a brothel.
taxi driver : you see there hookers outside pick anyone you like they will take you in.
will gets out of his cab and starts walking towards the hookers.
taxi driver : come on man you got to pay. dont make me wait.
he goes near the hookers.
the hooker asks wanna spent some nice time.
william : im looking for a girl. with a english acccent.
hooker : why you dont like american. [points at a girl] there she is .
william goes near her. she notices him coming towards her.will watches her face he, she is not jeny.
the english girl : you looking for something. mate.
will : im looking for a girl. she is been forced to live here.
the english girl : do you really thing we are forced to do this ?
will removes the picture of jeny from his jacket and shows the picture of the girl, "is she here. her name is jeny she is from notingham." [the pimp watches him showing picture to the girl]
the english girl : [the girl looks at picture]no mate, i have not seen her around. maybe you should try near the club micado. lot of english flesh around. you might get lucky there.
william starts walking to wards his taxi and the taxi drivver watches him. he starts his cab and goes near him.
the pimp comes near the english girl and in belly and asks. "what that guy wanted bitch "

the english girl has bended due to the punch and in pain answering :
he was looking for some girl, i told him try at some other place.
the pimp calls on his phone and says : looks like we got a finder.
william gets in the cab and says "take me to the club micado"
taxi driver : sheat, but you have to pay me first.
willl : why ?
taxi driver : beacuse you are looking for some serious trouble. [and drives the car]
they reach near the micado club.
taxi driver : well, here's your death station.
will : here's your money.
taxi driver : one advice, go back where you came from.
will gets out from the cab and the cab goes.
will goes near the hooker uot side of the club and starts asking about the girl.
and there is different pimp and he was talking on the phone after watching will : i tthink i found him.
he signs his fellow bad guys to follow him. 2 bad guys follow him
the pimp comes near the will and puts his hands will's shoulder. and starts walk with him.
the pimp : i think we found what you are looking for. but it will cost you.
the pimp : let me bring the girl first. [walks him in a dark street]
suddenly the pimp hods his neck tight and the guy from thee right removes a knife and tries to stabb him and he holds his hand and twists. and kicks him. the guy falls and the knife slides far from him.
he hits in the belly of the pimp with his left elbow. the pimp doesnt leaves his neck he hits him again.
the other bad guy from back hits above will's calves and will gets on his knees.
the pimp pushes him on the ground and they all start kicking him.

there comes the cop arrives on the next street and they run towards them.

the pimp watches the cop car warn's william : if i see you around the these girls again. it will be last thing you will ever see [the pimp snatches his picture from his jacket, kicks him and runs away]

there comes a taxi with the english girl in it. she stops near william.

the girl: get in before you get caught.

william tries to get up. the cops are about to catch them. will gets up and gets in the cab.

and the cab leaves.

the cab driver : good to see you alive trouble seeker. i knew this was gonna happen to you.

william trying to recover from his pain.

cab driver : where to mam.

the girl : just keep driving i'll tell you the way.

wiliam : where are we going.

the girl : to my house.

cut to

the pimp takes the phicture of the photograph from his cell phone and everyone. gets the message. dang, the pimps and the guy with the lizard tattoo also gets the meaassge.

cut to

the english girl enters her house. and she welcomes william. in the hall her friend was watching an action movie in full sound.

the english girl to her friend :keep it little low.

her friend : you came early [she was chewing on a gum and making balloons]

the english girl : yeah we ran from the cops.

her friend : we decided we wont bring customers in to our house [after watching william]

the english girl : he is not a customer.

her friend lokks at them going in the room and akes baloon from her gum and increases the tv volume again.

cut to

william sits on a chair.and the english girl goes for ice. she walks towards the fridge and start speaking.

the english girl : what were you thinking. you will get killed out there. the streets are dirty

she comes with the ice and gives him.

william takes it and puts it on his head.

the english girl : whats youur name

william : smith, howard smith.

the english girl : the girl from the picture. who is she.

william :stares and says nothing.

the english girl : i just saved your life buddy. let it be.

the english girl ; next you dont tell the story, i know everthing, the girl came here and she went missing. maybe she wants to live the american life.

william : jenny , never came here on her own. she was brought here.

the english girl : ohh my god she was abducted. [and gets shocked]

william : yeah from her house in notingham , what happened.

the english girl : abducted girls you will never find on the streets. they are sold on high price to buyers. your girl maybe history.

william : what do you mean by that.

the english girl : i was abducted too from great britain and was sold to a club owner in los angeles. we have to pleasure all the owners friends and customers after their card game. but night during the card games the owner got shot. and we all we free.

william : then why didnt you go home.

the english girl in anger : go home for what, my own family sold me. [and breaths heavy for 3 seconds and william stares her] i was only 15 when they sold me.

william still staring.
the english girl : when the club got shut, i had no where to go, somehow i managed to come here and dealed with the pimps. but i stand cant forget the horrors in the ship containers.
william : wait a minute you were brought from the ship from uk to L.A. i dont get it.
[he takes a paper and a pencil and draws a map of uk and america]
william : this is where you were taken and you are saying you were brought here crossing the north atlantic ocean then south atlantic ocean and then south pacific ocean and then you were brought here . [drawing lines on the map from the pencil]
the english girl : yes i was brought dirrectly to a port and then we were throwed in a truck and in 3 hours drive few girls were brought to the club.
william : i dont get it. how can they afford this.
the english girls : because there wasnt only girls. there were men to become slave, childrens to handle drugs and women for their dirty work.
william stares at her.
the english girl : and the uk ship was not the only ship,
william : then
the english girl : there were 3 more ships from other countries. with prisoners.
william : i still didnt get your ship part, if the ship is coming from united kingdom. the nearest port will be new york. or washington. and then you could have been transported from the road ways. why turn around so much.
the english girl : because each terrotery has a lord pimp. [she takes the pencil in the hand and marks] i was delivered to the pimp lord of L.A. and if your girl is brought to pensylvania then your girl must be delivered to the pimp lord who controls the nearest port like new

york.

william : so to find the girl i have to find the lord. [gets up and starts walking towards the door to leave the house]

the english girl : its not that easy. they have their secret ports, cops, they own everything for christ sake. atleast now tell who the girl is.

will looks at her for a second and leaves.

william comes out and watches the same taxi guy. he goes near the taxi.

the taxi driver : i figured you wont stay long.

will gets in.

the taxi driver : tell me your destination sir.

will : take me to the new york port.

the taxi driver : yes sir, [to himself] he is man on a mission. [starts the car and drives]

cut to

taxi driverdrives

sunrise shot

william sleeping. in the cab.

willliam getting visions.

of the english lady.

his daughter in blood.

pirates.

pimps.

cut to

william getting vision in front of the eyes ; caost guard saving him saying "are you there sir, can you see me'

cut to

the taxi driver : get up sir, get up.

william gets up and watches at the taxi driver.

william : where are we.

the taxi driver : we have reached at our destination sir. we are in new

york port.
william gets out of the cab [long shot] and camera pan to the new york port.
cut to
william getting in the port voyagge. watches around. a friend named robert find him. [there is too much rush in the port]
robert : hey will, what its been a long time [he hugs him]
robert : oh my god you look drained. were you sailing.
will : no. i left sailing. robert i need a favour.
robert : tell me what is it.
will : not here lets go somewhere private. [long shot]
cut to
they both are sitting in a coffee shop.
robert : you got be insane man. you are risking your life for a girl, who you dont even know. on the base of letters and a photograph you cannot find that girl. this proves nothing. you need more facts.
will : i only need where are the secret ports.
robert : you havent forgotten havent you.
will : i dont know what are you talking about.
robert : look if this is about the past. then i was with you too.
will : [screams] but you didnt see what i saw.
robert : calm yourself, you are getting drowned day by day. alright 2 miles from this port a place called black point that is a secret port, where illeagal goods are been smuggled. but im not sure if thats the port you want.
will : alright thats enough.
robert : what are planning to do. wait for them. such deals are not made everyday. they are made twice or thrice a year. are you gonna wait there that long.
will : how can we know when its happening.
robert : no one can tell when its gonna happen, but one thing you can

do is there is a pub where all the truck driver wait and drink till their shipment arives. maybe you can talk to some driver overthere you might get some information.

will : what is the club called

robert : its called the all's club.

will goes in that club, goes near the bartender and sits on the table.

will to bartender : [will gives some money] hey, i need some guy. who can pick up some stuff from the black point.

bartender shouts : hey fellows, this guy gives me a hundred dollars and say's wants to pick up stuff from the black point.

whole crowd laughs.

bartender throws his money.and says no one is available creep.

cut to

bartender comes out to throw garbage outside behind the bar.

will attacks him from behind. pushes him on the wall, and grabs his neck and twists his hand.

will : quite a good show you out in there. how about now sholud i break your neck or your hand. [twist his hand hard]

the bartender shouts huhhh !

will : tell who drives for the black point.

bartender : i'll tell you only if you leave me.

will leaves him and he coughs.

bartender : i thought you are a reporter man. i didnt wanted to get in any kind of trouble.

will : tell me who drives for it.

bartender : black point is secret. no one is allowed to talk about it. if anyone does he is dead.

will : who runs it.

will : what you know about the shipment few months back.

bartender : everyone know about this shipment. the drivers from my bar never ttake part in this sheat . we all know what the goods are.

will shouts fuck !

will : do you know how many innocents are trapped in this sheat hole.[breatths heavy]

bartender : but i think i know a man who can tell you. he has gone crazy after the shipment.

will : who.

bartender : his name is john. he was a happening guy, even though he was in depts. but after that night he is not the same person anymore. the man speaks with himself. talks to no one. cries alone. he is just too lost.

will : i know that feeling. where can i find him.

bartender : he comes here every night, he has the flame stickers on his truck.

will is sitting the club in front of the bar counter and having shots. and john enters and comes near the bartender asks for a shot. bartender signs will rom his eyes that he is john.

bartender to john : well hi john, how was your ride, you look tired john.[john takes the shot and lights his cigerette.]

john : lord himself is tired of us. i wonder where he goes to calm himself. [takes the taquela bottle] put me in my tab.

john goes on a table and starts drinking.

will watches john then , watches the bartender.

the bartender signs go for it, will goes towards john and sits on his table.

will : hi john.

john is wearing his cap and hidding his eyes with his neck down . john doesnt answers.

will : i got a shipment to deliver.

john : package and destinaation [his head is still down]

will : package cannot be revealed. but the destination is black point till pennsylvania.

john looks at will and takes a shot. again he looks down and smokes.
john : black point nevver heard of it.
will : atleast you know pensylvania.
john still looking down.
will : john you know what im talking about. i need ur help to find this girl. you know where she is.
john is still looking down.
will : atleast look at the picture.
john looks at the picture and says "take that picture out of my face"
will is still the picture in front of him.
john yells loudly : i said take that picture out of my face [shouts loudly and pushes his hand with the picture away from his face]
will : keeps the photograph in his pocket and says "i got my answer john " and leaves from there.
cut to
will wakes up the driver from the cab.
will : get up you slept enough. we got some work to do.
will and the taxi driver were waiting for john's truck to pass.
during this time will was smoking and drinking.
as johns truck passes. will wakes up driver again.
will : get up, thats our guy.
driver : this one. i got you thunder truck.
they starts following him. till where he lives.
ddriver : i dont know what the story is but i get a feeling you are in a good side. im with you man till its over [while driving]
and will watches him and stares at the running truck
john stops his truck and enters his house. will and the driver stops and watches his house.
taxi driver : what next sir. should we go inside
will : [will looks at the driver] no, we wait. [and looks at the house]
taxi driver : you sleep for sometime i'll watch him.

will : im not much into sleeping lately. like to keep my eyes open. [and watches at the house and the camera zoom on him]

cut to

one lady playing violin in a room and she is nacked and a crown sword on her hand.

pimp lord in a meeting with the buyer of men, women and children. surrounded by his masked bodyguards.

one guy : i need men, more men to work in my factory.

one more guy : yeh i girls more russian girls. how long will it take to for your next delivery.

pimp lord : this is not a easy business to run. one mistake can bring all our business down. you will get your goods. just have patients. there is a form in front of you. fill your requirments. and write your name down the form. you will get your goods as soon as possible. [there is a form which say men women and children and numbers in columns]

everyone starts filling the form.

and passes the papers to the pimp lord and he gives it to dang.

pimp lord : now when the business is done we feast.

there comes naked women with food and drinks and the pimp gets up and says enjoy your meal gentlemen.

the pimp lord leaves the room and dang follows him. and by the door.

the girls are cheering and the men are being naughty.

lord : did you find the girl.

dang : yes sir she died on the street. there will be no problem.

lord : huh good news, do one thing. send the girl with the violin in my room.

the girl watches him and tears in her eyes.

lord and dang watching her.

close up shot of the girl

cut to

day time. william watching john's house. and driver is slept. john

comes out.
will wake driver: get up we are on.
john take the truck and moves.
driver watching him leave. starts the car.
will : what are you doing.
driver : following him.
will : no, we break in.
will and driver comes near the house. stands in front of the door.
the driver rings the door bell. and the bell rings
will stares at him.
driver looks at him and says wotrth giving a shot.
driver turn back and will kicks the door.
will is searching inside. papers and documents. and also the drawrs.
driver find some some in the closet
driver : he i found some money.
will stares at him.
driver : arent we suppose to rob this guy. ok i will keept it back.
will is going through the documents. in front of the mirror, he finds nothing.
he looks in the mirror. a comic cover was sticked on the mirror. he picks it up.
and starts writting on a page the scratched letters.
driver : whats that
will : my house address from cambridge.
driver : how did it came here.
will : take me to new york.
cut to
a drunk guy from the bar came to the mansion. to inform about will.
the bodyguards takes him to the dang.
the drunk guy : i've got a tip for the lord.
dang : what is it

the drunk guy : i'll speak only to the lord. he might reward me for it.
dang gives him some money and tell me know.
the drunk guy : tohh this is not enough.
dang : let me see if your tip is worthy.
the drunk guy : there was a stranger he wants to know about black point.
dang : so this your tip. get him out of here.
the drunk guy : this is on the only thing. he came with the picture. and he is up to a driver named john.
dang : john who, the guy with the cap.
the drunk guy : yes you got it. thats the guy.
dang : where it happened.
the drunk guy : in the all's clubs.
dang goes in deep thought for a second.
the drunk guy : now where's my reward.
dang looks at him says to bodyguard. give him his reward and they walk him in the dungeons.
the drunk guy : where are you taking me.
the bad guys : you want to meet to lord dont you.
the drunk guy : yes yes it will be a grat honour.
the drunk guy watches cages in front of him and as he turns back dang puts a hot stamping rod in his eyes and takes the money back from his pocket and tells his guys to clean this mess.
cut to
will goes to new york port to meet robert.
their conversation on the port.
robert yells : a gun [looks right and left and says] what are you up will. how can i get you gun.
will : you know the place around here. there might be some way you can get me a gun.
robert : listen you dont stop this madness, i will inform your wife

will catches his collar : dont dare drag her into this.
everyone watching them from the docks.
robert : leave me, come on.
will looks here and there and starts breathing heavy.
robert : alright there is a way, yo u go down town, you might get a gun there.
and robert give him some money
robert : heres some money. this deal wont be cheap.
will : im sorry, robert. i didnt really mean to.
robert : its ok will, i owe you my life. now listen to me very carefully.
robert naration : get down town, you go there in a bar named mughal chong. you get in there will be people playing cards. tattood people, not good people. you have to play with them first then do the highest bid. let them know you got money. and them some drinks. they are greedy bastards they will ask you. you need something to buy something. then the play is yours. [visuals: will gets out of hhis taxi and gets in the bar and the taxi goes away, will enters the bar. has a drink and then walks towards the card game and asks may i play a hand. he play. he start making high bids. and looses. orders them drinks saying "shots for everyone" the guy with lizard tattoo in the hand asks, do you want to buy something mate. drugs, woman]
will replies : you got anything for protection. maybe be a knife or something. the streets are not safe.
tattoo guy laughs : i like this guy man, come on i got you something.
will gets in the toilet with him.
a guy comes with a gun in a bag and gives to the tattoo guy and he shows him to will.
the tattoo guy : check this out colt 45, easy to load easy to aim.
will [takes gun in his hand] : isnt it too rusty.
the tattoo guy : better than nothing.
will watches at the gun and thinks.

the tattoo guy : come one, i'll throw the bullets for free.

will : alright i'll take it.

cut to

will gets in the cab and tugs his gun in his jeans and keeps the bullet in his jacket.

the taxi driver : a gun, this is some bad news sir. where to now now sir.

will : take me to the all's club.

they drive.

cut to

sunset shot

top shot of cab

will and driver stops outside the all's club.

the driver looks at the johns truck and says" the truck driver is still here "

will : now thats none of your problem, you are free to go. here's the money.

driver : what you want me go when the real action starts. i dont want the money. you dont like my driving.

will : things might get rough from here. i cannot risk your life in this. take the money and go home. [will comes out of the car]

driver : come on is it my driving, you didnt like my driving. come on man this is not done [yelling and watching him go in the bar]

dang gets in the cab in the back seat.

the driver : i cannot go, its occupied.

dang : thats what i thought. [and puts a cotton on his face]

cut to

will enters thhe club take a shot watches john where he is sitting. and starts walking towards him. the bartender is watching him.

will comes near the table and throws the comic cover page on his table .

john watches the cover and say " you broke into my house'

will : because the letters carved in the page is my home address. you better start tallking.

john looks around and says not here.

cut to

they walk outside the club.

will : you better start giving some answers.

john : look man, im innocent . im just the truck driver. i tried to save the girl. i was the one who was sending you the letters.

will : where did you make the drop.

john : i cant tell you man. if i tell you im dead.

will removes his gun and catches him and points the gun on his head. and says " you are gonna die anyways "

there comes the dang with bad guys and shouts how about you both die

john : these are the guy's

dang with his guys had machine guns in their hands and start shooting.

john and will starts running towards the bar.

dang and his gang continues shooting.

will and john enters the club

dang and his gang shoots at the club too. watching this bartender says "i knew this was gonna happen"

will and john runs towards the window where the truck is parked.

dang and his friends enter the club and starts shooting everyone.

will breaks the window from his gun and they both jump out of the window and gets in the truck. and they run from there.

dang and his gang watches them go and shoots on the truck but they are long gone.

cut to

john and will stops at a beach.

john and will comes out.

john : fuck man, i am screwed. im dead now.

will : who were those guys.

john : you wanted to know, who took your daughter. those are the guys. go and ask them where is she.

john : i am dead man. i have no where else to go.

will : not if, you do as i say.

john : do what.

will stares at him.

cut to

both in the truck and john driving.

john : do you think this willl work.

will : trust me it will.

john : this people owns the police, policticians, street everything even the air we breath.

will : then why did you get into this. why did you sended me the mail, even though you did the drop.

john : its a long story man, 2 years back my father died. and left me this truck. and i was in dept i, in return they asked me for the truck. i couldnt just do it. i feel my father is alive in this truck. so they gave me an option of the drop. i thought it would be easy. but no. the drop took my soul with it. i tried to save your girl too. but they took her. i thought i right thing to do is to mail you. but im not able to sleep man. it just keeps on coming to me.

will hears it and looks outside.

will : looks like we all have our ghosts.

long shot of truck going

cut to .

will buys a video camera.

hides his truck with the tree bracnches near the mansion.

will and john climbing at the walls of the fence of the mansion. and

watches dang is gathering people with machine guns and starts getting in their suv's
john : looks like they are going out to hunt some one.
will : not some one us.
dang and his guys goes out of the mansion with guns wills starts recording . john and will jumps in the mansion from fence.
they go through the dungeons. john is filming and will is with gun.
they enter near the cages. they watch no one is there.
will watches the crown stamping sword.
john calls him : mr. smith
and will turns around and watches . the driver is tied to the chair with barbwire and will watches it and john films it.
the driver was was covered with his own blood and will recoginizes him .
john : ohh sheat, who is that guy.
will puts his hand on the camera and puts it down. as if stop filming to john.
will opens the cage and runs towards the driver, john follows him.
will tries to remove the barbwire. from his hand the driver shouts huuuh in pain and he looks up.
will watches his neck is also tied with barbwire. and blood is coming.
driver watches him.
will : hey boy, im here now. dont you worry
john : you know this guy.
will : yeah.
driver : sir i gave them nothing, they tried a lot. but they failed and left me here to die.
will tries to remove his barbwire from his neck. the driver shouts and start screaming. and his scars start getting whorst.
john stops will from doing it by nodding his head no.
driver : finish this sir. you have to end this. release me from this pain.

will : yes, yes im gonna get you out off here. [and tries to remove the barbwire and the driver shouts and john stops him]

john : this is not he means.

will stares at john and then to the driver.

will points his gun on his head.

driver : you didnt tell, how's my driving.

will : you did good boy [and hugs him]

will points the gun on his head and looks away from him and shoots and there were sparks from the gun.

the gunshot is heard by the pimp lord, the maids working in the mansion and even the bodyguards.

the pimp lord to his bodyguards : go and check what's going on.

will in anger starts walking inside the hoouse to find the people behind this.

john takes his camera and keeps it in his jacket. and starts following will.

will was entering a door and sudenly one bodyguard comes in front of him. will catches his machin gun from left and hits his head from a revolver. and keeps on hitting.

one more bodyguard comes and start shooting from his machine gun. will hides behind the bodyguard.

will shoots from his revolver, the sparks come and his hand get too shaken beacuse of the gun.

the second bodyguard gets shot.

the gun falls from the hand of will. and he screams wacthing his hand. 'ohhh fuck '

dang gets a call they are in the mansion. dang turns the car and goes towards the mansion with his bodyguards

first the maids run and the 3rd bodyguardd comes at shooting them. and will takes the maachine gun from the first dead bodyguard. and starts shooting.

john picks up the revolver and the spark and the jerk to his hand happens to him too.

more bodyguards come. starts shooting at them.

john again picks up the revolver. and tells will "we have to fall back they are in a big number.

john and will starts running backwards then will shoots people who are after them.

they run towards the dungeon and from there they run out. and climb the fence and jumps out.

and runs into the bushes. and gets in the truck. will stops him from starting the truck.

will : wait, wait for sometime.

on the main road will watches the dang and his bodyguard pass.

will says now

john starts the truck and they both go from there.

cut to

dang and his bodyguard linned up in front of the pimp lord.

pimp lord : the rats have reached the house. and made holes in this beautifull house. time to burn down the house. but just remember if the house gets on fire. you are getting burnned alive with it. find the rats and cage them. before its too late.

dang relpies yes sir. and dang exits from there.

cut to

john while driving the truck " ohh my hand "

john : fuck man you are hell of a trouble maker.

will : are you sure we can trust this people.

john : relax she is desperate for such work.

cut to

they both ring a bell at womans door.

the woman opens the door

john : miss shabana. i need your help.

miss shabana : do you know what time is it.

john : its really urgent.

miss : alright come in.

they eneter .

will watches her articles all over in her house. rescue girls from iran. women employerment. article in magazine.

miss shabana watches the video and says, " there will be a police inquiry, but doesnt proves that they are involved in human trafficking. "

miss : the owner of the house is mr. albert dimitry, as john told me before. he followed a shipment and the drop was here.

will watches john that he lied to her.

miss : from that time im on him.

will : atleast you can get for this guy tied in the chair.

miss : he will be charged with abduction, oor torture. and he might simply deny and manipulate like people who broke into his house has planted this. he is a very powerfull man.

will : mam, here's the chase im looking for my girl jeny. she is been abducted from the house. [he gives her the photograph of jenny]

miss : what is your name and did you even get this far.

will : my name is howard smith and its complicated. can you just help me get the girl back. he has the girl. we got to grab his neck.

miss : i have her picture and let me see. and you guys never showed up here and we never met. i'll tell the police someone has put this eveidence outside my door. but im gonna need more proof. that dimitry is behind this flesh trade.

will [drinks the whiskey] : im on it. [will and john gets up and starts going towards the door]

miss : be carefull and be in touch, looks like you guys are gonna do something stupid.

cut to

john to will : im on it, what did u even mean by that , what are we gonna do next mr. smith. i cant see a way to find the girl.
will : do you remember that sign the iron stamp. the crown symbol. what did it mean.
[they both get in truck]
john : how would i know. feels like shoot dimitry myself with this broken gun, where did you even get this gun.
will : i bought it.
john : sure they made a fool of you. who was it [starts the truck]
will : a guy from new york, russian maybe. tattoo'd a lizard tattoo on his wrist.
john stops the truck and stares. will also.
john : tattoo over here on the wrist [shows from his hand]
will : how did you know.
john starts the truck : buckle up we have a long way
cut to
the lizard tattoo guy playing cards with his friends in the same bar and will and john enters the bar.
the tattoo guy : hey look who's here.
will walking fast towards him. will takes his gun out and start beating his head and shoots his friends and keep on beating him and doesnt let him speak.
cut to
sunrise
john's house. the tattoo' d guy has been brought to the john's house. he is tied on a chair and his face been covered.
will removes the cover from the face.
the tattoo'd guy : seriously for a gun. you took this far.
will shows him the photograph of jenny : whhere is she.
tattoo guy : i dont know man, i have never seen her before.
will [beats him asks]: look at her, again.

tattoo guy : no, i dont know what are you talking about. i really dont know her.

john : i have seen you, helping the mob in black point.

tattoo guy : it was job, its not i have ordered the girls. we were suppose to be only on the port to help them load.

will : where do they send the girls.

tattoo guy : evereywhere . the buyers are from everywhere. i have only heard but never seen. the buyers start bidding and the highest bidder gets the prize. then the girls are transfered to guy who bought them. we only deliver the package. we dont sell them. [visual buyers buying in the dungens and the tattoo guy watching it and delivering the package to the owner from their truck]

will : where did you deliver this girl. this girl was not for sale. she was not there at all. [will punches him] you are a liar.

tattoo guy : im not lying, to save my self i will give you buyer. but she was not there. trust me.

john : i think he is telling the truth.

phone rings john hgoes to pick up.

miss shabana : john the lord is been is in custody.

john : did he talk.

miss : no, he denies, the poliice checked the house. the house is also clean, no sign of the guy. not a single drop of blood.

miss : there is one more thing, i always double check the victims.

john : so what did you get.

miss : i got nothing about the girl. but i got on howard smith. few days back he and his friends went out for a night drive and he never returned.

john : offcourse because he came here to find the girl.

miss : thats what fears me, howard,s car was found in the lake. there was no body found. when i went through the pictures. he is not howard smith. he is someone else. wait im sending you the picture.

john watches the real howard smith picture.and even his passpot, identy card picture.

john watches the picture and watches will. john goes near will.

will to tattoo guy : what is the meaning this crown sign.

tattoo guy : crown sign, you mean the iron stamps on the girls.

will : yeah, what does it mean.

tattoo guy : it means they are keeping the girls for themselves. when the girl is marked, she stays with the lord. that's all i have to say, i have nothing else.

will takes the knife and puts on tattood guy's neck

will : then there's no reason for you stay alive. [and was about to cut his throat, but john takes the gun tell him to stop.]

john : stop, i wont let you kill more people. tell me who are you.

will : im smith the girls father.

john : [shows the pcture from his mobile] no you are not smith, he is.

will cuts the throat and say's "so you know"

john watches the tattoo guy die and says "stop right there, who are you and what do you want"

will : you wont belive.

john : you better start talking.

will : i took a new house and one day i got your letter. and i figured that howard smith has sold his daughter here. so i killed. and i came here in the search of a girl.

john : you are making this up. tell me what her freedom got to do with you.

will : [yells] because im caged before. i know the horrors what i have been through. it was a time when i was working in transport of good. and i was travelling from the south atlantic ocean

cut to

cargo ship in ocean

robert and will on the ship of cargo. will is ordering his men.

will to a guy : look that container was not suppose to be there. [pointing at the cargo]. what is it even doing there.

robert enters : let it be will its done you cannot go back.

will : but dont know what is inside . it was not suppose to be on the ship.

robbert : now you are gonna do what. dump it in to the ocean. no one can do anything. just relax. enjoy the waters. we will figure when we port.

inside the container there were men hidding with guns. they were the pirates.

as they turn. pirates from the container come out. and starts shooting. they kill many loaders.

will to robert : so we will figure when we stop. [starts running towards the captain.]

robert : how was i soppuose to know what is inside.

they both starts running and pirates are taking over the ship.

will goes near the kicthen and tell robert to hide in the meat freezer. they will never find him there

will enter the captains cabin.

will to captain : its an hijack.

capatain on radio : mayday, mayday. we are under an attack.

the pirates enter the cabin and tells the capatin to stop the ship. captain only watches him in fear. the pirate shoots a guy and say's "stop it now".

they line up everyone the boss of the pirate enters. with his ship.

boss : well what do we have here goods. raw materials.

will : yes take it, what ever you like

boss : what will i do with the goods. i need money.

capatain : there is no money, only good. you might sell them.

boss shoots the captain : i assume that was the captain. [asks the william on gun point]

william : yes he ws the captain.
boss : that means, no one can move this ship. i know this ship has no money, no oil, only goods. but your governnment has it. make a call and arrange money. or you will be sinking with this ship.
cut to
on the news an anchor showing maps and videos of the hijacked ship. and they are asking 10 millon pounds in return of the ship and the crew.
everyone are watching the news.
the extraction team goes to the ship after planning and plotting and they reach the ship and shoot all the pirates but there was no sign of the crew.
the boss from his ship gets the news about the rescue team.
will was caged in that ship with the rest of the crew. there was a chest. will checks it.
will to a loader : you get in the chest. they wont even figure out how many are here. you stay there until i say.
the loader get intoo the chest and boss enters and to hide robert will sits on the chest.
boss : looks like your government denied to pay. at least we wont be empty stomack for few days.
the boss stabs a big sword into a loader and all his intestines comes out.
will and the crew starts running towards him but the pirates grabbed them and tied on the sealing of the cabin.
boss : cook him good and feed them too.
the guy was getting coocked in front of them and they were watching.
when everyone goes will asked the loader to come out. the loader comes out.
will : untie us.

the loader unties everyone.
the loader : lets run out of this ship.
will : we cant, the water and the cold will kill us. we have to take over the ship.
one pirate enters and watching them untied he gets shocked. the crew grabs him and beats him. and will grabs his gun and tugs in his pants and takes hhis sword.
suddenly the boss shoots at will in the shoulder.
boss : looks like the bird are free. what was your next move take down the pirates and and take over the ship. the smell of freedom. we been looking for. the only way your gonna get out this ship is we eat you nd we sheat.
the pirates laugh.
boss to will : you the captain of this crew. you are gonna die last. you think of your self as a peter pan, but this aint a fairy tale. burn one of them alive. [and boss leaves]
they tie them all and burn the hidden loader alive and the pirates make them watch.
will naration ; we watched him burned alive and eaten. i was 3 months in that sheat hole. they eat my crew one by one. they even made me eat my own friend. there were only 3 of us left. but we knew we are not gonna live long. [visuals they taking one by one and cutting them and eating them. pirate forcing will to eat beating , stabbing will and torturing him and boss pissing will from above the cage. and laughing on him.]
will is tied on the roopf his cabin. and due to a sea wave jerk will falls down.
and a pirates comes and starts beating him and wills visions are blurry. the pirate puts his head on the log and was about to decaptivate him. but ssuddenly there was a gun fight outside and will sleeps on the floor where there was all blood.

the pirate gets shot and the u.k. coast guard puts torch in his eyes this one is alive.

coast guard to will : can you hear me sir. are you there.

cut to

will with john and john listening to will

will : i lived till this day, but dead long back. i know what is meant to be caged. its whorst than dying.

john : how should i believe you.

will takes the johns phone and shows him the hijack and wills rescue story in the internet.

will : i only hidded my name for the sake of my family.

john was watching the article and suddenly he gets a call from miss shabana, john picks up.

miss : i got the girl, but there is a bad news she is dead. we checked on the orphan dead people and she was recognized by the hospital. she was found on the street but couldnt make it till the hospital. im sending you the loccation. and what about the fake mr. smith.

john : he is clean, im sending you the article. but keep it a secret.

john keeps the phone.

john : there is a bad news.

will stares

cut to

the truck stopped near the location and they both gets out. they walk towards the beggar on the street.

john : this is the location.

will goes near the oldman who spoke during the passport burning.

will shows him the picture.

will : did you now this girl.

oldman : yeah but she is dead.

will : i know. i want to know about her.

oldman : the girl was thrown here by some guys. she was not usefull for them. she got pregnant. the girl lived on the street eating garbage. i helped here. i even wanted to help her go home. buut she came to know that her own father sold her. [visuals flashback]

will : but how did she died.

oldman : one night agroup of junkies came in. i was hidding her. but they caught her and dragged her and they stabbed her many times . [visuals junkies grabbing and trying to rape her and they figure she is pregnant but still they rape her. after raping the junkies run and her condition gets serious the oldman stops a car ask them to call the ambulance]

oldman : next thing i came to know she didnt make it.

will : did she had anykind of mark in her body.

oldman : yes she had a crown mark on her wrist. but i never asked.

[visual oldman watching crown mark on jenny]

oldman : who are you, and why are you asking for her.

will : my name is howard smith.

oldman slaps him

john : hey oldman, what the fuck

will stops john from talking

oldman : say's leave from here before i kill you.

will gets up and starts walking

the olman shouts your gonna burn in hell howard smith.

john : looks like the name you chose has been cursed. [they both get into the truck]

will : i got to live with that.

cut to

will, miss shabana and john sitting in the coffee shop.

miss shabana : its finished we cannot do anything. he got way from the guy from his house as well.

john : im dead anyways.

will : i will kill dimitry first.

miss : it wont do any diference. there are plenty of guys to take his place. i wanted him to get caught in the act. so can pull down his buyers as well. i wanted to break his back bone. i wonder what happens to the child.

will and john stares at each other.

will : hat child.

miss : jenny was pregnant, the baby still lives in the hospital.

will : we got dimitry now.

john : how.

will : what did the tattoo' guy said about the mark.

john : yeah dimitry keeps his girls marked.

will : and what did the beggare said .

john : jenny had a crown mark on her wrist.

will : and the girl was pregnant.

john : this means dimitry is the father of the baby.

miss : all we need is a dna test. i 'll go to my contacts and police for the dna test of dimitry. and you guys quick go to the hospital.

will an john stares

miss : because he will try to kill the baby. [gives the details of the baby in a paper] this is where the baby is [john takes it]. and william. its william isnt it.

will nods his head yes.

miss : your secret is safe with me.

will nods his head and both runs towards the truck

miss calls the police and says we have to take the dna of dimitry.

police : is there a problem.

miss : i will explain you later.

police ; ok mam [she cuts the phone and the policeman is standing in front of dimitry and and dimitry smiles]

cut to

john and will talking in the truck.

will : speed up, we have to reach the hospital as fast as possible.
john : the cops are gonna be any moment there.
will : thats what worried about.
john : so whats the plan.
will : we have to take the baby and get to new york.
john : whats there.
will : a ticket from out of here. you are coming too. but frist we have to get the baby.
john : so what do we have.
will : wwe have a mchine gun with no bullets. a jerking revolver with few rounds.
john : [stamps on the dashboard] dont worry, i have my father.
cut to
dang is with weapons in his suv wih his gangbangers. and heading towards the hospital. total there are 4 suv
cut to
john sending message on his phone.
will : who are you texting.
john : just calling for the back up.
cut to
miss and police at the dimitry house for the dna test.
dimitry : smilling at the miss.
cut to
dang and his gang stops at the hospital. from 2 car gang gets out and starts walking towards the hospital.
john with his truck smashes 2 suv and the guys in the car. and say's i missed them.
dang and his gang starts shooting at thhe truck.
they come out from the otherside of the truck.
the people in hospital gets scared.
from the smasheshed suv. they grab the machine guns and start

shooting back at them.
dang stops few gang members at the the gate gate of the hospital.
it was imposible to take down theose guy's from the gate so will goes under the truck and shoots their legs. and john shoots them.
they enter the hospital.
john : its in the 3rd floor.
will and john starts starts getting to the child ward and dang catches a doctor and asks on his gun point where the babies are delivered.
the doctor replies on the 3rd floor.
dang reaches near the baby.
one of the gangbanger : should we shoot the baby.
dang : the babby never existed. just grab him.
the gun fight between the mob and the john.
will shoots the guy who had baby and john grabs the baby.
will gets out of the bullet.
will runs towards a guy and while fighting with him hand to hand they both fall from the window.
now john is all alone and running out with the baby. he gets shot and stabbed many times. but somehow he comes out.
willl watches him coming out he shoots the man running behind john
there comes the bartender with his car.
bartender : come on in for christ sake.
will comes down and gets in the car. will watches john is shot.
they drive. dang get in with his guys and follows the van of bartender.
will : john are you ok.
john : just grab the baby. [and takes the gun and shoots from the window]
bartender : john just hang on , let me get on the highway.
bartender gets on the higway and the truck drivers smashes dangs and his gang's car.
will : where did came from.

john : this was not the only back up i called.
they reach at new york port. the cops are following them.
will : john lets gets out of here.
john is dead.
bartender watches and say's ohh john. you better get going. otherwise all of this for nothing. the cops surround the van, and the van is empty.
cut to
robert is getting in a boat towards the sea with will and the baby. and hhdding them under the blanket.
cut to
on news channel
dimitry getting arrested. [anchor speaking]
the girls from dimitry's house released.
even the cops involved getting arrested.
his buyers getting arrested.
the girls, children and men getting released and send back to their home.
casualties of taxi driver and john in this act.
there is a man behind it. he is going to appear in court today. he got letters at his house this where a;ll began. lets take you live from the court.
will speech : there are people who are caged againt their will. there are more victims of this acts. everywhere around the globe. release them. let them go free. [visuals crowd, girls, wife and mrs. smith watching him live]
everyone deserves a home. let the poor souls get back to their home or will be coming for you. my name is howard smith and make sure i dont get a mail again.[picks up the news paper where taxi driver and john's photo is . watches it and leaves the court]
will comes outside keeps walking.

miss shabana comes there and says dont worry about the baby she will be fine, and gives him the passport. its done mrs smith.

will keeps on walking. and his daughter watches him on t.v. she says hey its daddy.

eli : no my sweet child, he only looks like your father. he is howard smith.

cut to

will in plane. airhostress gives him a drink. saying mr. smith your drink.

will in the streets near his house.

will comes near the oldlady.

oldlady : so how was your trip .

will : it was good.

old lady : so mr. smith, new name, new house whats next.

will walks towards his mail box and checks.

the old lady stares at him.

will watching her smiles.

the end.

written by yogendra nikale

Contents

9 798887 335964

Printed by Libri Plureos GmbH in Hamburg, Germany